This Walker book belongs to:

_____

_____

_____

For Alexandra May

First published 2007 by Walker Books Ltd
87 Vauxhall Walk, London SE11 5HJ

This edition published 2008

10 9 8 7 6 5 4 3 2 1

This book has been typeset in Cafeteria Bold.
Handlettering by Colin McNaughton.

Printed in China

British Library Cataloguing in Publication Data: a catalogue record
for this book is available from the British Library

ISBN: 978-1-4063-1241-6

www.walker.co.uk

Nighty night!

Colin McNaughton

WALKER BOOKS
AND SUBSIDIARIES
LONDON · BOSTON · SYDNEY · AUCKLAND

said Littlesaurus.

"Yes," said Daddysaurus.

"It's time for bed."

"I want a story!" said Littlesaurus, and he put his pyjamas on.

So Daddysaurus told him
a funny story.
"Ha-ha-ha, he-he-he!"
laughed Littlesaurus and he jumped up
and down on the bed.

"Daddysaurus!"

said Mummysaurus. "You're supposed
to be calming him down."

"Nighty-night, Littlesaurus," said Daddysaurus.

"I'm not tired," said Littlesaurus.

"What if I sing you a lullaby?"
said Mummysaurus.

"Hmm," said Littlesaurus,
"that might work."

But it didn't.

"I've got a tummy-ache!"
said Littlesaurus.

So Mummysaurus rubbed
it better and said,
"Now, try to go to sleep."

"But my bed's all itchy,"
said Littlesaurus.

"Go to sleep," said Daddysaurus.

"But I –" said Littlesaurus.

"Sle

ep!"

said Mummy and Daddysaurus.

"BUT I can't help it if I'm not tired and I don't want to go to sleep because it's not dark outside and ANYWAY I want a glass of milk and there's a SHADOW on the wall and I want ANOTHER story and I've got an ITCH and ANYWAY my friend Whippersnappersaurus says he can stay up all night long if he wants to and ...

ANYWAY why can't I stay up as long as Bigsistersaurus and I'm too hot and my tummy hurts again and nobody loves me and I HATE school and ANYWAY when Nanasaurus babysits me she reads me HUNDREDS and MILLIONS of books and tells me funny stories and tickles me and I LOVE her and I'm hungry and I think there's something under the bed and I've got a wobbly tooth and

CAN I GET UP?"

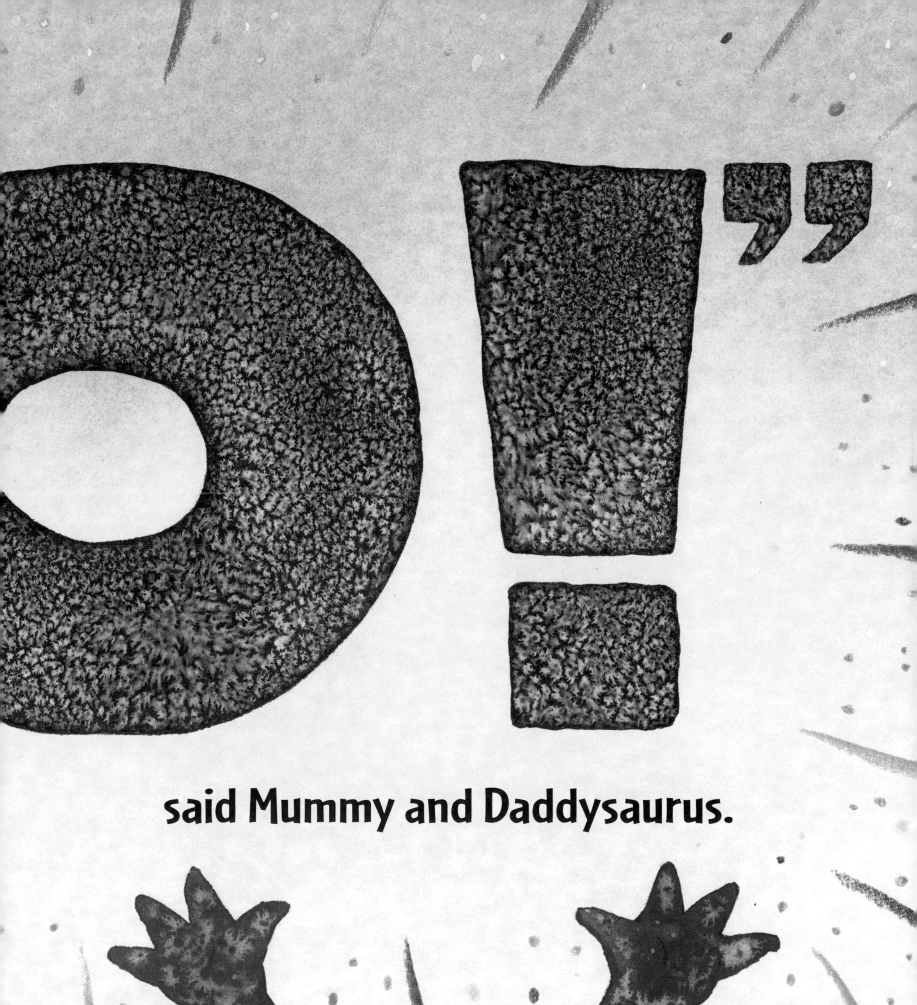

said Mummy and Daddysaurus.

said
Littlesaurus.

But that's not the end of it because Littlesaurus waited until Mummy and Daddysaurus were snoring and then he snuggled in between them.

And guess what?
He went straight to sleep.
Nighty-night!

Other books by
Colin McNaughton

Here Come the Aliens!
ISBN 978-0-7445-4394-0

We're Off to Look for Aliens
ISBN 978-1-4063-0645-3

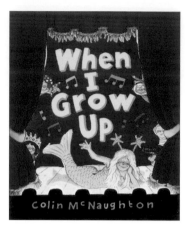

When I Grow Up
ISBN 978-1-4063-0041-3

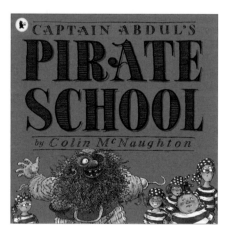

Captain Abdul's Pirate School
ISBN 978-0-7445-9896-4

Captain Abdul's Little Treasure
ISBN 978-1-4063-0585-2
(PAPERBACK AND CD)

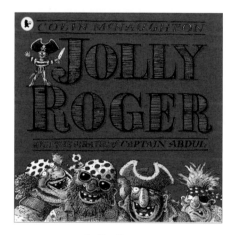

Jolly Roger
ISBN 978-1-84428-478-8

Available from all good bookstores

www.walker.co.uk